# FOLKT *from* Ecosystems
### Around the World

Retold by
Claire Daniel

### Illustration

Dennis Hockerman
"The Lonely Lioness"

Diana Magnuson
"Pedro and the *Frijole* Pot"

Red Hansen
"Ian Ho and the Wise Man"

Marilee Heyer
"Pepito and the *Chirimia*"

Laura Jacobsen
"The Return of Summer"

**STECK-VAUGHN**
ELEMENTARY · SECONDARY · ADULT · LIBRARY

A Harcourt Company

www.steck-vaughn.com

# ❧ Contents ❧

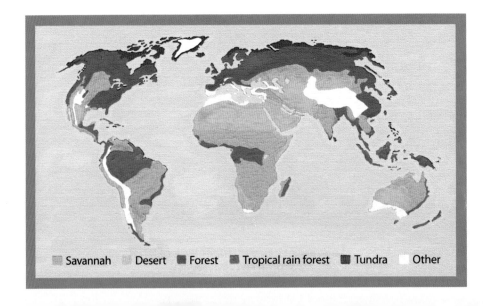

Savannah    Desert    Forest    Tropical rain forest    Tundra    Other

# The Lonely Lioness
## A Folktale from the African Savanna

*D*eep in the southern part of Africa lies a rolling grassland called the savanna. It is a place of tall grasses and few trees, of heavy spring rains and long, dry summers. Long ago on this savanna, there lived an old lioness. Many rainy seasons had come and gone since her last cubs were babies. Now grown into lions, they brought fresh meat to Lioness each day because she was too old to hunt. Even worse, Lioness was almost totally blind. The golden grasses that covered the savanna in summer were a yellow blur to her. Giraffes walking in the distance looked like floating brown poles. Knowing that she would be unwise to wander, Lioness stayed close to an acacia tree.

One summer afternoon Lioness rested peacefully
under the acacia tree. She sniffed the breeze that carried
the smell of the golden grass that stretched out all
around. Soon her four sons would bring her a fresh
meal, and she drooled a bit, just thinking about it.
Her eyelids drooped, and Lioness soon fell asleep.
She dreamed that she was young and strong and her
sons were cubs once more.

At the same time that Lioness napped, Ostrich led
her little chicks to their watering hole, which shrank a
little bit more each day. Rain had not fallen for some
time, and none was expected for another few months.
Ostrich dug in the dirt around the pond, finding little

to feed her children. Then she spotted some nice, juicy grasshoppers. They would make a wonderful meal! One by one, she fed the grasshoppers to her chicks.

"Slee, smee, slee!" the first chick said as she ate a big grasshopper.

"Sluck, smuck, sluck!" the second chick said as he swallowed his fat meal.

"Slurp, smurp—burp!" the third chick said and then added, "Excuse me!"

"That was delicious!" the fourth chick said after swallowing her grasshopper. "Now can we play in the grasses?"

"Yes, please!" the other three chicks chimed in.

Ostrich was now very hungry herself. She spied a mouse near the water. She thought about what a nice meal the mouse would make. "Go along," she said. "I'm going hunting."

The chicks began chirping and running in circles. Ostrich ran toward the mouse. The mouse was very quick, so Ostrich ran farther and farther away in search of her prey. As she followed the mouse, she thought, *I should have told the chicks to stay away from the lioness who lives by the acacia tree.*

Left on their own, the chicks scattered every which way, playing hide-and-seek in the tall yellow grass. Farther and farther from the watering hole they ran, hiding and chasing. Finally the four chicks found themselves standing exactly where their mother did not want them to go.

The chicks' chirping woke up Lioness, who yawned widely and blinked. She stared at the chicks and cried, "My babies! You've come back to me!" As she nuzzled each one, she said, "How handsome you all are!"

The chicks did not know what to say. None of them had never seen a lion before and did not know to be afraid. Like most babies, they did not have a very good memory, either. They quickly accepted Lioness as their mother and forgot all about Ostrich.

Ostrich finally caught the mouse and swallowed it in one bite. Then she found a gecko, a fine meal for her chicks. She carried the gecko in her beak and followed the trail of trampled grass her chicks had left behind. Suddenly she stopped dead in her tracks. The gecko dropped from her beak. Directly ahead stood the acacia tree. And under it her four chicks were playing with the Lioness.

Ostrich's blood ran cold as she watched Lioness purr and coo at the chicks. *Lioness thinks my chicks are her babies!* Ostrich realized.

Ostrich wanted to go get her chicks, but her heart was full of fear. When Lioness was younger, she had almost caught and eaten Ostrich. The chicks' mother was scared to go near the huge cat.

Just then Ostrich spotted Aardvark, who was heading toward a huge mound full of tasty termites. Ostrich stopped him and said, "Please help me! Lioness has taken my babies. She thinks they are her cubs! Please help me get them back!"

Aardvark was hardly more than a baby himself, but he agreed to help Ostrich.

"Oh, thank you, brave Aardvark!" Ostrich replied.

"But what exactly do I do?" asked Aardvark.

Ostrich said, "You must reason with her. Point out how skinny the chicks' legs are. She will realize that they are not her cubs. Then she will let them go."

"Very well," Aardvark said, and he ambled over to the acacia tree. He spoke to Lioness. "What beautiful babies you have!"

Lioness was licking their feathers. "Yes, they are," she said proudly.

"But what skinny legs they have! I believe these babies are not lion cubs at all."

Lioness's horrible roar knocked Aardvark off his feet and sent him rolling across the savanna. "That's ridiculous!" she snarled. "These cubs will soon grow. When I bring them meat, they will eat, and their legs will grow fat. Now be off with you!"

Ostrich watched Aardvark run away. She didn't know what to do next. She had to get the chicks away before Lioness's four adult children returned. They would eat her chicks in four gulps.

Just then Gazelle trotted by. Ostrich stopped her. "Please help me!" she begged. "Lioness has taken my children! She thinks they are her cubs. Please help her see that the chicks are not her babies."

Gazelle thought for a minute and then agreed to reason with Lioness. She approached Lioness and said, "What a nice brood of cubs you have!"

Lioness purred. She gathered the chicks around her and nuzzled their feathers. "Yes, they are quite lovely," she said.

"There is only one thing wrong," Gazelle said.

Lioness growled low in her throat.

"Don't you think it's odd that they have feathers and not fur?" Gazelle asked cautiously.

Lioness sniffed. "Don't be silly! The fur on small cubs is always feathery!"

Gazelle started to argue, but Lioness snapped, "Get out of my sight!"

Gazelle smiled at this last remark because Lioness clearly could not see. How could she get out of Lioness's sight when Lioness had no sight? The more Gazelle thought about what Lioness had said, the funnier it seemed. Gazelle tossed her head back and let out a little laugh.

Lioness's sight was not good, but her hearing was perfect. "How dare you laugh at me?" she roared at Gazelle. "You won't be laughing when I tear you apart!"

Gazelle didn't want to anger Lioness any further, so she followed Aardvark, who was still running away from the acacia tree.

Ostrich paced back and forth and flapped her wings. She was very upset now because she knew that Lioness's sons would soon reach the acacia tree. Just then Mongoose trotted past, and Ostrich asked him to help.

"Absolutely! I am happy to help you!" he said as he puffed out his chest.

Lioness was not surprised at Mongoose's courage. Everyone knew that Mongoose was not afraid of any animal on the savanna.

Mongoose approached Lioness and the four chicks. By then the chicks were tired and had fallen asleep in the grass. Lioness was curled up around them.

Mongoose said loudly, "Those are the ugliest lion cubs I have ever seen! If I were you, I'd roast them and feed them to the elephants!"

Mongoose chuckled to himself. He knew that elephants didn't eat lion cubs—or ostrich chicks, either, for that matter.

But Mongoose didn't have time to laugh very long. Lioness was so angry that she sprung off her haunches and lunged toward him.

Mongoose was so quick that when Lioness landed where he was standing, he was long gone. Lioness lumbered after him, but her jaws met only with the dust from his tracks.

Meanwhile Ostrich quickly gathered her four chicks and took them far away from the acacia tree. And there the chicks stayed and lived four very long lives on the savanna. When they grew up, they told their children to stay away from the acacia tree and to be careful around lions. Then they told their chicks the story of the lonely lioness who slept under the acacia tree, dreaming of her four cubs.

# Pedro and the Frijole Pot

## A Folktale from the North American Desert

Long ago a farmer named Pedro lived in the Sonoran Desert of Mexico. The Sonoran never receives much rain, but one summer only a few inches fell. Pedro's underground well began to dry up. Day after day he stood in the hot sun and watched his corn and *frijole* plants slowly die.

Pedro saw that he had two choices. He could stay on his farm and hope that rain would fill his well once again. Or he could move to another place where there was water for his corn and beans.

Pedro decided that moving was better than hoping. Early one morning he packed his few clothes, some dried *frijoles,* a bedroll, and some gourds full of water.

He also packed his *frijole* pot and the small amount of gold he had left. This money was all he had, but it was enough to buy a new farm with fresh water.

Pedro soon found that he liked camping in the desert. He liked searching for the precious aloe plant, whose juices soothed his sunburned arms. He liked looking at the rugged Sierra Madre mountains off in the distance. He even liked watching scorpion babies ride on their mother's back.

During the day, he often stopped walking to watch a woodpecker drill a hole in a giant saguaro cactus. He searched the skies for a glimpse of a hawk. He watched roadrunners dash in and out of the rocks and scrubby brush that covered the Sonoran.

At night Pedro made camp. He laid out his bedroll and made a campfire from branches of paloverde and mesquite trees to keep the coyotes away. He ate *frijoles* that he had cooked that morning. Then he lay down and gazed up at the stars in the clear desert sky as he listened to the coyotes howl.

One night three mule drivers saw Pedro's fire and surrounded him. Pedro was a little scared because there were so many of them and they looked so rough.

Pedro thought about his gold, which he had hidden under his *frijole* pot. Thinking that his money was safe, he relaxed a bit.

That night the mule drivers sat around Pedro's campfire and talked until Pedro could stay awake no longer. Finally he climbed into his bedroll and fell fast asleep.

As Pedro was sleeping, the mule drivers tore up the camp, looking for the money they knew he must have. Finally they found Pedro's bag of gold coins under his *frijole* pot.

The mule drivers did not know they had awakened Pedro during their search. Pedro watched in silent horror as they stuffed his money bag into their bags. Then after a minute, Pedro smiled. What the mule drivers did not know was that Pedro was smart and that they had met their match. Pedro closed his eyes and went back to sleep.

Early the next morning, Pedro got up before the mule drivers stirred. He rolled up his bedroll. Then he dug a shallow hole and built a fire in the bottom of it. When the fire was very hot, he placed the *frijole* pot on the coals. The pot became very hot. Pedro picked up the pot and covered the hot coals with a layer of sand. Then he replaced the pot on the hidden hot coals. Last, Pedro put *frijoles* in the pot with some water and began to cook them.

When the four sleeping mule drivers smelled Pedro's *frijoles* cooking, they sat up in a flash. "That smells delicious!" they said as they gathered around the pot. Pedro said nothing as he stirred the *frijoles*.

The head mule driver licked his lips. "What are you making?" he asked.

"*Frijoles,*" Pedro replied.

Then the head mule driver looked more closely at the pot and exclaimed, "Look at that pot! It is cooking on bare ground without any fire!"

Pedro smiled. "Yes. That's because it is a magic pot."

The mule drivers licked their lips. Then one said to another, "We must have this pot. If we didn't have to look for wood to make a fire each day, we could save a lot of time."

"You must sell us that pot," the head mule driver said to Pedro.

Pedro said, "I could not do that. I need it."

"You know we could steal it from you," the head mule driver said as he looked at Pedro long and hard.

Pedro said, "You could, but the pot would not cook for you. It works only for me."

The mule driver slowly stroked his chin and asked, "How much money will it take to buy that pot from you?"

Pedro named a sum that equaled the amount they had stolen from him plus the cost of a new *frijole* pot.

"It's a deal!" the mule drivers said.

Pedro stood up and said, "Listen carefully to me. I will stir the *frijoles* once more and tell the pot to cook. Then I will pull away. While I am pulling away, you take the spoon and stir. The pot will think you are its master and obey you."

"*Bueno!*" the mule drivers said.

Pedro stirred the pot once more and said, "Cook, pot, cook!" He handed the spoon to the head mule driver, and the driver stirred the *frijoles*.

"Cook, pot, cook!" the driver ordered the pot.

The pot was still hot, so Pedro quickly packed his things and slipped away while the mule drivers talked excitedly about their magic pot. When Pedro was out of the mule drivers' sight, he ran as fast as he could.

That evening the mule drivers pulled out the *frijole* pot and put it on the sand to cook their supper. The head mule driver put *frijoles* and water into the pot and said, "Cook, pot, cook!"

Of course, nothing happened. "We've been tricked!" the mule drivers cried. They searched for Pedro and his money for days, but they never found him.

Pedro traveled across the Sonoran until he found a farm that he could afford. There was a creek with plenty of water for his crops, so he planted corn and beans. Pedro became very comfortable and lived quite well for all the rest of his days. Of course, he bought a new *frijole* pot, and each morning he used it to cook a batch of *frijoles* as the sun came up over the desert.

# Ian Ho and the Wise Man
## A Folktale from the Asian Forest

Ian Ho was the youngest child in his family and grew up with four brothers. His mother chose his name because it meant "goodhearted and interesting," and she favored him. The other four brothers were very selfish and not at all interesting. They were jealous of Ian Ho, so they took care to torment him when their mother was not looking. They told him more than once that he was not smart and that he would never amount to anything.

Ian Ho must have believed his brothers, because when he was twenty, he found himself friendless and poor. He only had one coin left, so he went to the market to buy a piece of fruit to fill his empty stomach.

An old woman in the market pulled Ian Ho aside. "You will find happiness and fortune if you visit the old man who lives on top of Mount Jiri," she said.

Ian Ho shook his head at her foolishness and started to walk away. Mount Jiri was surrounded by wild forests and filled with danger. *I will surely be killed if I make the trip*, he told himself.

She called after him, "The trip will not be easy. You will climb difficult paths. The journey will take you ninety-three days. If you seek happiness and fortune, you must go now."

Something in the old woman's voice made Ian Ho stop. He gathered the few things he owned and began walking toward Mount Jiri.

Soon Ian Ho had reached the edge of a great forest with oak, maple, and birch trees. He spotted deer and an antelope. He had never seen such wildlife in the village where he grew up! Not long after, Ian Ho walked past a tiger, but it paid no attention to him. Ian Ho's heart sank. *I am so worthless that even a tiger ignores me*, he said sadly to himself.

A month passed, and Ian Ho became content eating nuts, mushrooms, and berries he found in the forest.

It was autumn, and the leaves on the trees had turned to deep gold and red and orange. Ian Ho came to love the peaceful beauty of the forest and its animals. He hummed to himself as he traveled onward.

During the first month of his journey, Ian Ho had seen no human being, so he was surprised one day when he came upon a little house tucked away in a stand of pine trees.

A young woman named Mira opened the door and invited Ian Ho inside to eat and to rest. She saw that he had very little, but that did not bother her. She was glad to have his company. When he turned to leave, he thanked Mira and asked her what he could do for her in return for her kindness.

"Oh, please ask the wise man on the mountain when I will no longer be lonely," she replied.

Ian Ho agreed, and soon he was again on his way. He hiked up a long hill covered with spruce and fir trees. Fallen needles lay thick on the ground like a soft carpet. At night Ian Ho slept under a tree and dreamed of the young maiden.

After another month, he reached a raging river that cut through the forest. The river was too dangerous to cross, and Ian Ho wondered how he would get to the other side. Just then, a huge dragon rose from the water. Ian Ho wanted to run, but the voice of the dragon stopped him. The dragon asked Ian Ho where he was going. When Ian Ho answered, the dragon said, "I will carry you across the river," in a deep rumble.

Ian Ho hopped on the dragon's back. After the two reached the other side of the river, Ian Ho thanked the dragon and asked the dragon how he could repay its kindness.

The dragon said, "I have everything a dragon could want. My gold coins and necklaces outshine the sun. My ruby is as big as a duck's egg and burns with scarlet fire. The only thing I really want is to fly. I have tried and tried, but my wings won't work. Will you please ask the wise man when I will be able to fly?"

Ian Ho agreed to the dragon's request and walked on toward Mount Jiri. After another month, he came upon a cottage in a grove of mulberry trees. Two apple trees stood on the north side of the cottage. An elderly couple walked out to meet him.

By then Ian Ho's coat was so torn that it hung on him like rags. The man gave Ian Ho a new red cloak, and Ian Ho thanked the couple for their generous gift. When he told them where he was going, they grew excited, for they had heard that the old man of the mountain was truly wise. Because the couple were so old, the journey up the mountain was too difficult for them to make. Ian Ho asked them what they would like to know from the wise man.

They asked, "Could you ask him how we can make our apple trees bear fruit? We planted them ten years ago, but we haven't seen one apple yet."

Ian Ho agreed to help the couple and again went on his way toward Mount Jiri. On the ninety-third day, he reached the base of the mountain. He climbed over rock after rock. The path was so steep that he had to pull himself up by the roots of small evergreen shrubs that wound in and out of the rocks and soil.

When Ian Ho reached the top of the mountain, the wise man was waiting for him. "Welcome, Ian Ho! I have been expecting you!" the wise man greeted him. "Tell me about your journey!"

Ian Ho told the old man about the couple with the two apple trees that would not bear fruit. Then he described the dragon and asked the wise man when it

would be able to fly. Last, Ian Ho told the wise man about Mira. He asked the wise man when she would no longer be lonely.

The wise man said, "Tell the couple to replant the apple trees on the south side of the house. Then the trees will bear fruit. As for the dragon, tell him he will be able to fly when he is no longer greedy. Tell Mira that when she sees a person who makes her heart sing, she will no longer be lonely."

Ian Ho said, "Thank you."

The wise man smiled. "Ian Ho, haven't you forgotten something?" he asked.

Ian Ho replied, "What would that be?"

"Why did you come to see me?"

Ian Ho blushed. "I almost forgot." Then he said, "I wish to find happiness and fortune."

The wise man smiled and said calmly, "You already have. You will see what I mean by the time you return home."

Ian Ho did not feel all that pleased. He had wanted fortune and happiness that very minute. But he decided to trust the wise man, and he waved his goodbye with a faint smile.

Within minutes he reached the cottage in the mulberry grove. He told the couple they must replant the two apple trees on the south side of their cottage. They agreed, and the three of them began digging. When they dug up the two trees, they found a bag of gold under each! The couple were so grateful that they gave Ian Ho one of the bags.

Ian Ho continued on with his bag of gold. In another few minutes, he reached the raging river. "I guess it's true that the journey home is always shorter than the one away!" he said with surprise.

The dragon heard him speak and asked him what the wise man said about his flying. Ian Ho told him he had to let go of his greediness, and the dragon drew a pouch from under its wing. In the pouch lay the dragon's huge ruby. "This ruby is half of my fortune, and it is yours. Wish upon it, and you will receive whatever you want."

Ian Ho hopped on the dragon's back, and the dragon carried him to the other side of the river. Then the dragon flew away through the clouds.

Ian Ho looked at the red stone. He said, "I wish for a fine horse to take me home."

At once a white horse appeared beneath him and trotted to Mira's house. She ran out to meet him, and Ian Ho saw that there was no woman more beautiful.

Ian Ho told Mira, "The wise man said that when you meet someone who makes your heart sing, you will not feel lonely any more." He got off the horse and took Mira's hand. They both smiled at one another because they knew that both of their dreams had come true. They had all the money they needed, and they had each other.

Soon after, Mira and Ian Ho were married. Ian Ho built a fine home for them in the forest because he always wanted to remember his journey and its wonderful ending. In time he and Mira had many children who grew as strong as the oak trees and whose laughter filled the forest.

# Pepito and the Chirimia

## A Folktale from the Tropical Rain Forest of Central America

*T*here was once a time when the rain forest of Guatemala had no music except the sound of its songbirds. The loveliest of the birds that sang was the quetzal. The quetzal's song was so sweet that even the harpy eagle dared not eat it for fear of losing the beautiful music.

One day a little boy named Pepito was born to a poor but noble family who lived in a village in the rain forest. The young boy loved the sounds of the birds. When he was eight years old, he opened his voice to make a noise like them. He was disappointed to find that he could not imitate their sounds, but he was amazed to find that he could sing!

All the villagers were just as surprised. They had never heard anyone sing before, and they thought Pepito's musical voice was remarkable.

In another part of the rain forest, there lived the king of the Mayan people. He and his queen had a beautiful daughter named Keeyah. This daughter loved the music of the rain forest birds, too. Each morning she sat by her window and listened to their songs.

When it was time for the princess to marry, the king asked her what kind of man she wished to choose.

Keeyah said, "When he speaks to me, he will remind me of the birds in the rain forest."

The king called all the young nobles in the rain forest to come before him. He gathered them together in a large hall and announced, "I wish my daughter to marry."

The young men began talking among themselves. Everyone knew how beautiful and sweet the young princess was, and each young man longed to take her for his wife.

The king pointed to Keeyah and told the young men, "Speak with my daughter and tell her why you wish to make her your wife."

A hundred young men rushed to line up in front of the princess. They all pledged their love for her and described her beauty. Some begged. Clever ones quoted poetry. Men who could not speak well cried after they failed. Not one reminded the princess of the rain forest birds.

Pepito was the last young man waiting in the line. He had been pushed to the end because he was dressed so poorly and because he did not want to fight the others. No one thought he had a chance to win the princess's heart. When it was his turn, the poor young man walked forward. He stood and waited.

Impatiently the king said, "Well, get on with it! Speak up!"

Pepito was frightened by the king's gruff voice. He was so scared that he could not speak at all.

"Remove him!" the king yelled.

Seconds before the guards moved to take him away, Pepito opened his mouth and began singing. He sang a song of love for the princess. His voice was so sweet that the songbirds in the rain forest stopped to listen. Even the quetzal stopped singing to hear him.

Then Pepito finished. No one said a word, and not one bird made a sound. Pepito concluded that he must have made a big mistake, so he turned to leave before anyone could scold him for his performance. But before he took a step, the princess stood up and gently took his hand.

"That was lovely!" she said, looking at Pepito with wonder.

The king saw that the princess liked Pepito, but he didn't think a poor noble was good enough for his daughter. He stepped between the princess and Pepito. "That sound was beautiful, but it was not the sound of a bird," the king said.

"You are correct, father," the princess responded. She turned to Pepito and asked, "Can you make the sounds of the birds?"

Pepito looked down at his feet "I'm sorry, princess, I cannot," he replied.

"Then be gone with you!" the king said. He hoped that the youth would leave and never return. Turning on his heel, he began to walk away.

"No!" said the princess because she had already fallen in love with the young man, poor clothes and all. She looked at Pepito, then grabbed her father's hand and said, "Father, I have an idea. If Pepito can learn to make the sounds of the birds within three months' time, will you let me marry him?"

The king knew that her request was impossible, so he agreed.

Pepito walked into the deepest
part of the rain forest, where he could
listen to the birds with the sweetest songs.
For days he sat under the same mangrove
tree, listening to them. But when he tried to
sing like the birds, he still sounded like a person
singing.

After two months of listening, Pepito still was
no closer to making the sounds of the songbirds.
He sat under the mangrove tree and wept. That
was when the quetzal flew down to his side.
"What is the matter?" asked the quetzal.

Pepito explained, "I have one month to learn
the songs of the birds, and I will fail. I will never
be able to sing the way you and your fellows do."

The bird hopped on his shoulder and spoke. "You
are right," she replied. "You cannot sing like we do.
But there is another answer to your problem."

The bird told Pepito to cut a small branch from a
nearby tree. She showed him how to hollow out the
branch and carve six holes into one side of it. When
he had finished, the quetzal told Pepito, "You have
made a *chirimia*."

"What is a *chirimia*?" Pepito asked.

"It is a kind of flute," the bird said. "Go ahead, blow into it gently."

When he did, he heard a sound that he had heard before. It was a sound much like the birds of the rain forest. Then the quetzal showed him how to put his fingers over the six holes to make different sounds. What beautiful music the *chirimia* made!

Pepito had another month before he had to return to the princess. Each day the quetzal taught him a new song. Each day the cockatoos and macaws gathered to listen. The hummingbirds stopped beating their wings and listened, too. Toucans stopped eating figs so that they could hear the sounds of the *chirimia*. All the birds agreed that Pepito was quite good. Pepito kept practicing, and after a month his playing sounded just like the rain forest birds.

After the month had passed, Pepito said goodbye to the quetzal and the other rain forest birds. He returned to the king's palace. Pepito asked the king if he could perform for Princess Keeyah.

The king knew Pepito was sure to fail, so he eagerly agreed.

Pepito stood in front of the king, the queen, the princess, and the people of the kingdom. He brought the *chirimia* up to his lips. He blew the sweetest love song that had ever been heard in the rain forest. The palace filled with the sounds of the rain forest birds.

The song was so beautiful that the king and queen were very glad to have Pepito marry their daughter. Immediately they began preparing for the wedding celebration, an event that lasted for more than a month.

After Pepito so successfully played the *chirimia,* people from all over the kingdom wanted to learn as well. And from that day on, the Maya have enjoyed music of all kinds, but the *chirimia* has been the most popular musical instrument of all.

# The Return of Summer

## A Native American Folktale
## from the North American Tundra

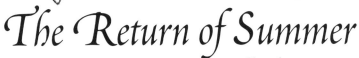

*E*arly one spring in far north Canada, just before the snow melted and the lakes thawed, a tribe of bears stole the warmth of summer. They packed it up in a bag and tore a hole in the sky. They climbed through the hole and closed the opening with a needle and thread.

On the earth below, the tundra animals suffered greatly. Without the warmth of summer, the days were long and cold. Clouds covered the earth. New snow fell over the old snow of winter and never melted. The ponds and lakes stayed frozen and held the fish in an icy grip.

The air was so cold that the mosses, grasses, and other tundra plants could not grow new leaves or flowers. Soon the plants began to freeze and die.

The caribou, musk oxen, ptarmigan, and other plant-eaters grew thin and weak from hunger. All the animals knew that if the plant-eaters died, then the meat-eaters would, too. Something had to be done soon, or all the animals would die of starvation.

The animals held a meeting to discuss the problem. Tundra Swan held a piece of thread in her beak. She dropped it in front of the other animals and said, "I know where the tribe of bears lives. I found the place in the sky where they hid the warmth of summer. They sewed up the hole with thread. I pulled out a bit of the thread, and now there is a small opening."

The animals decided to send a special team to take back the warmth of summer. Only the smallest of animals could squeeze through the hole. Only the fastest of animals could move swiftly enough to outrun the bears. At least one of the animals needed sharp teeth. All the animals must be able to move quietly. The animals chose Young Caribou to go because he was strong and fast but still small enough to fit through the hole. Wolverine, Arctic Fox, and Lemming were also chosen to make the difficult and dangerous journey.

Tundra Swan led the team of animals to the small opening in the sky. One by one, the animals squeezed through the hole. When they stood up inside the world above, they could not believe their eyes. The sun shone brightly, and birds sang. Green grass covered the ground, and wildflowers bloomed in the meadows. Large, ripe berries hung heavily from bushes. Fish jumped in and out of the deep blue lake. Insects buzzed among the tundra flowers.

Lemming said, "It's so beautiful and warm! I had forgotten what summer was like!"

Wolverine said, "Look later! We don't have a lot of time to waste."

The four animals walked to the cave where the family of bears lived. They pushed open the door and saw two cubs playing by a fire.

"Hello!" said Wolverine.

"Hello!" said the cubs. "Who are you?"

Wolverine did not want to tell them, so he changed the subject. "What a nice fire you have!" he said.

"Come and warm yourselves," invited one cub.

The animals walked in cautiously and looked around. They saw four large bags lying in the corner of the cave.

Arctic Fox pointed to the bags and said, "What is in those bags over there?"

One of the cubs said, "The first bag holds the rain. The second bag holds the wind. The third bag contains the fog."

Wolverine asked, "What is in the fourth bag?"

The other cub said, "We are forbidden to tell you that. Our mother would be very unhappy with us if we told you what she keeps in that bag."

Arctic Fox felt the bag. It was very hot. He knew that the bag contained the warmth of summer.

Wolverine motioned for the team to leave the cave and hold a meeting. They walked outside and discussed how to take back the warmth of summer.

Young Caribou said, "I will run around to the other side of the lake. Mother Bear will see me and try to catch me."

"But she will come after you in her canoe!" said Arctic Fox. "The lake is wide and deep. It would be easier to paddle across the lake than run around it. There's a good chance she might catch you!"

"Not if I gnaw on the handle of her paddle first!" said Lemming.

They all agreed that their plan was a good one, so Young Caribou ran to the other side of the lake. He munched on the green grass. At the same time, Lemming gnawed all around the paddle.

Mother Bear's hunting did not go well that day, and she returned to the cave without any supper for her cubs. The hungry cubs saw Young Caribou across the lake and yelled to their mother, "Look! A caribou! We're starving!"

Mother Bear jumped into the canoe so that she could quickly reach the caribou. But after she had traveled halfway across the water, the paddle broke in two where Lemming had gnawed it. One half of the paddle fell into the water. Mother Bear stood up in the canoe to grab the end that had dropped, and she fell in herself.

"WAHOO! WAHOO!" the animals on the shore yelled in celebration. So far their plan had worked.

Arctic Fox and Wolverine dashed into the bears' cave, and Wolverine quickly hoisted the fourth bag over his shoulder. Arctic Fox hurriedly grabbed the end of the bag that trailed onto the ground, and the two ran toward the hole in the sky.

By the time Arctic Fox and Wolverine were halfway to the hole, Mother Bear had reached the shore of the lake. She began running after Young Caribou, who by then was running as fast as he could toward the hole.

As Mother Bear chased Young Caribou, she saw Arctic Fox and Wolverine with the bag of warmth. She knew she had been tricked.

Lemming reached the hole in the sky at the same time as Arctic Fox and Wolverine. They motioned for Lemming to slip though first. She said, "No, the bag of warmth goes first, because it is most important."

Mother Bear watched Arctic Fox and Wolverine pushing the bag of warmth through the hole. She ran more seriously then and began to catch up with the four animals. They could hear her hard, heavy breath as she pounded straight for them.

"Hurry!" Lemming cried. "Push!"

The bag holding the warmth of summer was heavy and hard to manage. Wolverine, Arctic Fox, and Lemming had to push with all their might. Finally the three managed to shove the bag through the hole. It fell to the earth and ripped open. Warmth began to spread all around.

Arctic Fox climbed through and pulled Wolverine after him. Mother Bear was three feet away as Young Caribou glided through the hole. Mother Bear growled in frustration, and then she spied Lemming on the ground beside her.

"Well, you didn't slip away, miserable Lemming!" said Mother Bear. "You won't make much of a dinner, but you'll have to do!"

Lemming squeaked in panic.

Mother Bear reached down to grab her meal, but Lemming dashed through the hole and slipped back to the earth.

Tundra Swan had been waiting for Lemming on the other side of the hole. As all the tundra animals watched anxiously, she sewed the hole shut. Then she tied the thread into a knot so that the hole would not come open again.

The warmth of summer filled the tundra. The snow melted, the ice thawed, and little seeds began to sprout. Soon after, small bushy plants with flowers covered the ground. Insects buzzed among the leaves and grasses. Fish swam freely in the lakes and ponds, and all the animals grew strong once again.

The next winter, the warmth of summer again disappeared. At first the animals thought the tribe of bears had stolen it again. But when spring arrived, the warmth returned. Knowing that the warmth would always return to the tundra, the animals never worried about the warmth of summer again.